Disney's Aladdin

p

Long ago, in the ancient city of Agrabah, there lived a ragged but handsome boy called Aladdin. His best friend was his monkey, Abu. He was very poor and often became so hungry that he had to steal bread from the marketplace.

This book
belongs to:

_____

Abu

Jasmine

Aladdin

The Sultan

STARRING

Iago

The Genie

Jafar

This is a Parragon book
First published in 2006

Parragon
Queen Street House
4 Queen Street
Bath, BA1 1HE, UK

ISBN 978-1-4054-8322-3
Printed in China

But Aladdin was determined he would not remain a thief forever. From his makeshift rooftop home he liked to pull back the curtain and gaze at the Sultan's sumptuous palace in the distance.

"Someday, Abu, things will change," he sighed. "We'll be rich, live in a palace and never have any problems at all."

Meanwhile, within the walls of the Sultan's palace, time was running out for the beautiful Princess Jasmine. She made sure that every suitor who came to visit was chased away by her pet tiger, Rajah.

"The law says you must marry a prince before your next birthday," said the worried Sultan. "There are only three days left for you to choose a husband."

"The law is wrong!" cried Jasmine. "I don't want to marry someone I do not love."

With that, she unlocked the door to the dove cage nearby and watched the birds fly away. She longed to be free like them.

Early the next morning, Jasmine crept out into the palace garden disguised in a long cloak. She hugged Rajah.

"I'm sorry, Rajah, but I can't stay here and have my life lived for me."

With Rajah's help, she climbed over the palace wall and made her way through the bustling streets.

Seeing a hungry child, Jasmine picked up an apple from a stall and offered it to him. The Princess did not know that she had to pay the fruit seller, because she had never left the palace before. "Stop, thief!" shouted the man, rushing forward to seize the Princess. Luckily, Aladdin had seen everything and he leapt to Jasmine's rescue.

Aladdin led her to the safety of the rooftop. As he gazed at the beautiful girl, he knew he was falling in love.

Suddenly the royal guards stormed up the staircase and arrested Aladdin.

"Release him, by order of the Princess!" Jasmine cried, pulling back her cloak.

"The Princess?" gasped Aladdin.

"I would, Your Highness," said the chief guard, "but my orders come from Jafar." Then the guards dragged Aladdin away to the palace dungeons.

Jafar was the Sultan's most trusted advisor, but, unknown to the Sultan, he was plotting to take over the throne. Jafar had a golden scarab that was the key to the Cave of Wonders deep in the desert. Inside this secret cave was a magic lamp that would give Jafar the power he needed.

However, the Tiger-God that guarded the cave had told Jafar that only a Diamond in the Rough – someone whose worth was hidden deep within – could enter the cave. Jafar looked in his magic hourglass and saw a vision of Aladdin. He was the one!

Jafar disguised himself as an old man and went to the palace dungeon. He told Aladdin about the Cave of Wonders. Then he helped Aladdin escape through a secret passage and led him through the desert to the cave.

"Touch nothing but the lamp and then you shall have your reward," he promised.

Inside the cave, Aladdin and
Abu made friends with a Magic
Carpet. It flew them past piles of royal treasures to the place
where the lamp was kept. Abu caught sight of a magnificent
jewel in the hands of a giant monkey statue. Forgetting the old
man's warning, Abu quickly snatched up the jewel.

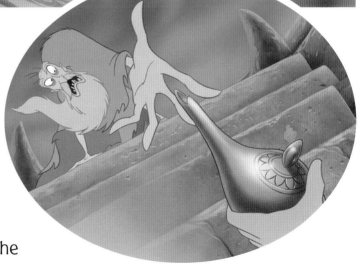

Suddenly the cave walls began to collapse and the floor gave way. Aladdin grabbed the lamp and the Carpet flew them back to the cave's entrance. The old man snatched the lamp from Aladdin's hands.

"At last!" he shouted, and pushed Aladdin and Abu back into the cave just as it sank into the ground. They were trapped!

Chittering happily, Abu produced the lamp. The clever little monkey had stolen it back from the old man!

"What's so special about this dusty old thing?" Aladdin wondered, rubbing it clean with his hand. Suddenly the lamp started to glow. A cloud of smoke billowed from its spout and a genie appeared.

"I am your Genie, direct from the lamp," said the amazing creature. To prove his powers, he told them to sit on the Magic Carpet, then they blasted straight out of the cave.

The Genie told Aladdin he had three wishes. Aladdin thought of Princess Jasmine. She would never marry a poor street boy.

"Genie," he said, "I wish I were a prince."

The Genie set to work, clipping, combing, shaving and trimming. In a few seconds, Aladdin was clean and smart. Then the Genie dressed Aladdin in the finest silks. He was transformed into a handsome prince called Ali.

Finally, the Genie turned Abu into a magnificent elephant. Then he conjured up a grand procession with musicians, fireworks and dancers. Prince Ali rode to the Sultan's palace in style.

"I have journeyed from afar to seek your daughter's hand," Aladdin said as he bowed before the Sultan.

That night, Aladdin crept up to Princess Jasmine's balcony.
He took her for a moonlit ride on the Magic Carpet. They soared
into the air, leaving the palace far below. Jasmine felt as free as
the birds that flew beside them. By the time they returned, she
knew that at last she had found a prince she wanted to marry.

But the evil Jafar had other plans. He wanted to marry the Princess himself, so he ordered his guards to capture Prince Ali and throw him off a high cliff.

As Aladdin sank beneath the waves, the lamp fell from his turban. Using Aladdin's second wish, the Genie saved his master from drowning.

Back at the palace, the wicked Jafar had hypnotised the
Sultan using his magical snake staff.

"You will marry Jafar," the Sultan ordered Jasmine in a
strange voice.

"Never! Father, what is wrong with you?" asked Jasmine.

"I know!" said Aladdin, bursting into the room. He snatched
the staff from Jafar and smashed it to pieces. At once the Sultan
snapped out of his trance. Jafar
fled. But as he left, he
spied the magic lamp
in Prince Ali's turban.

"So," thought Jafar, hiding safely in the tower, "Prince Ali is really that ragged urchin, Aladdin – and he has the lamp. But not for long!"

The next morning, Jafar's cunning parrot, Iago, flew silently into Aladdin's room and stole the lamp.

"At last! I am your master now!" cried Jafar, as he rubbed the lamp and watched the Genie appear. "Genie, grant me my first wish. I wish to rule on high, as Sultan!"

Reluctantly, the Genie obeyed Jafar's orders. Then Jafar ordered everyone to bow before him. When Jasmine refused he made his second wish. He wanted to be the most powerful sorcerer in the world.

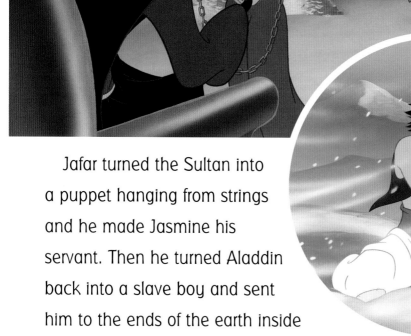

Jafar turned the Sultan into
a puppet hanging from strings
and he made Jasmine his
servant. Then he turned Aladdin
back into a slave boy and sent
him to the ends of the earth inside
one of the palace's giant pillars.

Luckily the Magic Carpet had sneaked inside the pillar and
was able to fly Aladdin and Abu back to the palace.

Aladdin's return
made Jafar even
angrier than before.

He imprisoned
Jasmine inside a giant
hourglass. Then he used
his magic powers to surround
Aladdin with a ring of sharp swords.
Aladdin bravely took up one of the
swords and challenged Jafar to a fight. In
reply, the evil sorcerer conjured up a flaming
wall of fire and turned himself into a cobra.

Jafar raised his snake head to strike Aladdin. "Did you think you could beat the most powerful being on earth?" he snarled.

Aladdin quickly thought of a way to trap Jafar. "The Genie has much more power than you!" he taunted.

The power-mad sorcerer knew that the boy was right. "Genie," he said, "my final wish is to be the most powerful genie of all."

A swirling mist of light surrounded Jafar and he changed into a towering genie.

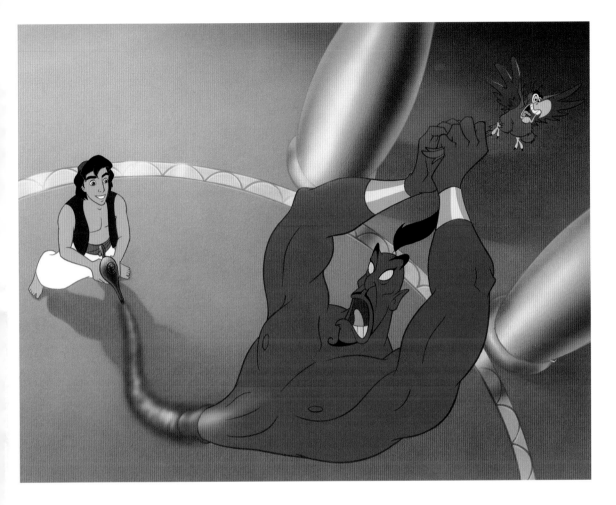

Then it was time for Aladdin to show Jafar his new home. He held up a tiny oil lamp and the new genie and Iago were sucked inside. Jafar's evil spell was broken.

The Princess ran into Aladdin's arms.

"Jasmine, I'm sorry I lied to you," said Aladdin. "I'm not a prince at all. I'm only the poor street boy you once met in the market."

"But I still love you," sobbed the Princess. "I want to marry you! Oh, if it wasn't for that stupid law!"

The Genie appeared at Aladdin's side. "You still have your third wish left," he said. "I can make you a prince again."

Aladdin shook his head. "Genie, with my third wish, I give you your freedom. But I'm going to miss you."

"Me, too!" the Genie replied with a smile. "You'll always be a prince to me."

"That's right," the Sultan agreed. "You have proved your worth. What we need is a new law. I decree that from this day, the Princess may marry whomever she wishes!"

"I choose Aladdin!" Jasmine cried in delight.

Aladdin took Jasmine in his arms. They knew that they would all live happily ever after.